SUDDENLY IN THE DEPTHS OF THE FOREST

Born in Jerusalem in 1939, AMOS OZ is the internationally acclaimed author of many novels and essay collections, translated into over thirty languages, as well as a children's book, *Soumchi*. His acclaimed semi-autobiographical work, *A Tale of Love and Darkness*, was a bestseller all over the world, and his most recent book was a novella, *Rhyming Life and Death*. He has received several international awards, including the Prix Femina, the Israel Prize, the Goethe Prize and the Frankfurt Peace Prize. He lives in Arad, Israel.

Suddenly in the Depths of the Forest

Amos Oz

Translated from the Hebrew by
Sondra Silverston

Chatto & Windus
LONDON

Published by Chatto & Windus 2010

2 4 6 8 10 9 7 5 3

Copyright © Amos Oz 2005
Translation copyright © Sondra Silverston 2010

Amos Oz has asserted his right under the Copyright, Designs
and Patents Act 1988 to be identified as the author of this work

First published in Hebrew as *Pitom Be-Omek Ha-Yaar* by
Keter Publishing House Ltd, POB 7145, Jerusalem, Israel

First published in Great Britain in 2010 by
Chatto & Windus
Random House, 20 Vauxhall Bridge Road,
London SW1V 2SA
www.rbooks.co.uk

Addresses for companies within The Random House Group Limited can be found at:
www.randomhouse.co.uk/offices.htm

The Random House Group Limited Reg. No. 954009

A CIP catalogue record for this book
is available from the British Library

ISBN 9780701182274

The Random House Group Limited supports
The Forest Stewardship Council (FSC), the leading international forest
certification organisation. All our titles that are printed on Greenpeace
approved FSC certified paper carry the FSC logo. Our paper procurement policy can be
found at www.rbooks.co.uk/environment

Mixed Sources
Product group from well-managed
forests and other controlled sources
www.fsc.org Cert no. TT-COC-2139
© 1996 Forest Stewardship Council

Typeset in Sabon by Palimpsest Book Production Limited,
Grangemouth, Stirlingshire

Printed and bound in Great Britain by
CPI Mackays, Chatham ME5 8TD

1

EMANUELLA THE Teacher described to the class what a bear looks like, how fish breathe and the kind of sounds a hyena makes at night. She also hung pictures of animals and birds on the classroom walls. Most of the children made fun of her because they'd never seen an animal in their lives. Many of them didn't quite believe there were such creatures in the world. At least not around here, they said. Besides, that teacher never found anyone in the whole village who wanted to marry her, they said, and that's why her head was full of foxes, sparrows, all sorts of things people think up when they're lonely.

Emanuella's descriptions had only a minor effect on the children, except for Little Nimi, who began to dream about animals at night. Most of his classmates laughed at him when, first thing in the morning, he told them how the brown shoes he'd put next to his bed before he went to sleep had turned into two hedgehogs in the dark and crawled around the room all night, but in the morning, when he opened his eyes, they were just a pair of shoes next to his bed again. Another time, black bats came to his room at midnight and carried him off on their wings, flew through the walls of the house up into the sky above the village and over mountains and forests till they brought him to an enchanted castle.

Nimi had a muddled brain and a constantly runny nose. He also had a large gap between his prominent front teeth. The children called that gap the garbage dump.

Every morning Nimi would come to class and begin telling everyone about a new dream, and every morning they would say enough, we're sick and tired of you, shut that garbage dump of yours. And when he didn't stop, they made fun of him. But instead of being offended, Nimi would join in the ridicule. He would breathe in his snot and swallow it, and brimming over with joy, would call himself the most insulting names the children had given him: garbage dump, fuzzy-brain, hedgehog-shoes.

More than once, Maya, daughter of Lilia the Baker, had whispered to Nimi from her seat behind him in class: Nimi. Listen. Dream about whatever you want, animals, girls, but keep it to yourself. Don't tell anyone. It just isn't a good idea.

Matti said to Maya, You don't understand. The only reason Nimi has those dreams is so he can tell us about them. And anyway, he doesn't stop dreaming even when he wakes up in the morning.

Everything delighted Nimi, anything made him happy: the cracked mug in the kitchen and the full moon in the sky, Emanuella's necklace and his own buck teeth, the buttons he forgot to button and the wind howling in the forest. Nimi found fun in everything there was and in anything that happened. And the least little thing was enough to make him burst out laughing.

Until the day he ran out of class, out of the village and climbed up to the forest alone. Most of the village people searched for him for two or three days. The police searched for another week or ten days. After that, only his parents and sister kept looking.

He came back three weeks later, thin and filthy,

3

all scratched and bruised, but whooping with joy and excitement. And Little Nimi has been whooping ever since and has never spoken again: he hasn't said a single word since he came back from the forest, he just wanders around the village streets barefoot and ragged, his nose running, baring his teeth and the gap between them, skipping from one backyard to another, climbing trees and poles, whooping all the time, his right eye constantly watering because of his allergy.

He couldn't go back to school now that he had whoopitis. On their way home, the children would whoop at him on purpose to make him whoop back. They called him Nimi the Owl. The doctor said it would pass with time: perhaps there, in the forest, something had frightened or shocked him, and now he had whoopitis.

Maya said to Matti: Shouldn't we do something? Try to help him? And Matti replied: No, Maya. They'll get tired of it soon. They'll forget about him soon.

When the children chased him off with their mockery and the pine cones and pieces of bark they threw at him, Little Nimi would run away, whooping. He'd climb the closest tree and from up in the high branches, he would whoop at them again with his one weepy eye and his buck teeth. And sometimes even in the middle of the night, the villagers thought they heard the distant echo of his whooping in the dark.

2

THE VILLAGE was grey and gloomy. Around it on all sides were only mountains and forests, clouds and wind. There were no other villages nearby. Visitors almost never came to that village and passers-by never stopped there. Thirty or forty small houses were scattered on the slope of the valley enclosed by towering mountains. The one pass through the mountains was on the western side and the only road to the village was through that pass, but it didn't go any further because there was no further: the world ended there.

Once in a great while, a travelling tradesman or pedlar, and sometimes just a beggar who had lost his way, would come to the village. But no wanderer ever stayed longer than two nights because the village was cursed: it was always eerily silent, no cow mooed, no donkey brayed, no bird chirped, no flock of wild geese crossed the empty sky, and the villagers barely spoke to each other beyond the essential things. Only the sound of the river could be heard constantly, day and night, because a powerful river rushed through the mountain forests. It passed through the village, white foam on its banks, frothing, seething and bubbling with a low roar, until it was swallowed up again in the bends of valley and forest.

3

A T NIGHT, the silence was even blacker and thicker than in the daytime: no dog stretched its neck and flattened its ears to howl at the moon, no fox whined in the forest, no night bird shrieked, no cricket chirped, no frog croaked, no rooster crowed at dawn. All the animals had disappeared from the village and its surroundings many years ago – cows and horses and sheep, geese and cats and nightingales, dogs and spiders and rabbits. There wasn't even one small goldfinch. Not a fish was left in the river. Storks and cranes bypassed the narrow valley on their journeys of migration. Even bugs and reptiles, bees-flies-ants-worms-mosquitoes-moths hadn't been seen for many a year. The grown-ups who still remembered usually chose to stay silent. To deny. To pretend they'd forgotten.

Years ago, seven hunters and four fishermen had lived in the village. But when the river emptied of fish, when all the wild animals drifted far away, the fishermen and the hunters left too and went to places that were untouched by the curse. Only one old fisherman who keeps to himself, Almon is his name, has stayed in the village to this day. He lives in a small cabin near the river and holds long, angry conversations with himself while he cooks potato soup for his meals. Even now, the people of the village still call him Almon the Fisherman, though he changed from fisherman to farmer a long time ago: during the day, Almon grows vegetables and edible roots in beds of crumbling soil and cultivates twenty or thirty fruit trees on the slope of the hill.

He even put up a small scarecrow in his vegetable beds because he believed that all the vanished birds and animals might yet return in his lifetime. Sometimes Almon has long, angry arguments with that scarecrow too, pleading with it, scolding it, giving up on it completely. Then he returns with an old chair, sits down in front of the scarecrow and tries with endless patience to win it over or at least persuade it to change its stubborn opinions, if only a little.

Towards evening, on clear days, Almon the Fisherman usually sits in his chair on the riverbank, puts on the old glasses that slide down his nose towards his thick grey moustache, and reads books. Or he writes and rubs out line after line in his note-book as he mutters to himself all sorts of arguments, opinions, reasons. And with the passing years, he has learned, by the light of his night lamp, to carve bits of wood into a great many beautifully shaped animals and birds and also unknown creatures that he saw in his imagination or in his dreams. Almon gives those carved wood-creatures to the village children as gifts: Matti got a pine cone cat and kittens carved from the bark of a walnut tree. For Little Nimi, he carved a squirrel, and for Maya, Almon made two long-necked cranes with wings spread and stretched out in flight.

It was only from those small carvings and the pictures their teacher Emanuella drew on the black-board that the children knew what shape a dog was and what a cat looked like, or a butterfly, a fish, a chick, a kid and a calf. And Emanuella taught some of the children how to imitate the sounds of the animals, sounds that the people of the village surely remembered from their childhood, before the animals disappeared, but the children had never heard in their lives. Maya and Matti almost knew something they were forbidden to know. And they were careful not to let anyone suspect that they knew or almost knew. Sometimes they met secretly behind the abandoned hayloft where they would sit and whisper for about fifteen minutes, and when they left, they each took different paths. Of all the grown-ups in the village, there was perhaps only one they could trust. Or not: several times Matti and Maya had almost decided to tell their secret to Danir the Roofer, who in the evening would sometimes joke loudly with his young friends in the village square about things that children were forbidden to hear. And when he drank wine with his friends, he was known to joke about a horse, a goat, a dog he was thinking of bringing from one of the villages further up the valley.

What would happen if they told Danir the Roofer their secret? Or maybe they should tell old Almon instead? And what if, one day, they dared to go a little way into the darkness of the forest to try to find out if their secret was real or only an illusion, a passing dream that Nimi the Owl might have, but certainly not them?

And meanwhile, they waited without knowing what they were actually waiting for. Once, towards evening, Matti bravely asked his father why the creatures had vanished from the village. His father was in no hurry to answer that question. He stood up from the kitchen chair, paced the room for a few moments, then stopped and grasped Matti's shoulders. But instead of looking at his son, the father's eyes wandered to a bare spot on the wall above the door where the plaster had crumbled because of the seeping dampness beneath it and said, Listen, Matti. It's like this. Once, things happened here in the village, things we're not proud of. But not everyone is to blame. Certainly not to the same degree. Besides, who are you to judge us? You're still a child. Don't judge. You have no right to judge the grown-ups. And anyway, who told you that there were animals here once? Maybe there were. And maybe there weren't. After all, so much time has passed. We forgot, Matti. We forgot and that's it.

Leave it alone. Who wants to remember? Now go down and bring some potatoes from the cellar, and stop asking questions all the time.

As he got up suddenly to leave the room, Matti's father said one more thing: Listen, let's agree on one thing, you and I – that this conversation never happened. That we never even talked about it.

Almost all the other parents chose to deny it. Or to avoid the whole subject by keeping silent. Not to talk about it at all. Especially not in front of the children.

4

S ILENTLY AND sadly, the village lived its simple
life.

Day after day, the men and women went out to
work in the fields, in the vineyards and orchards, and
in the evening, they would return wearily to their small
homes. Every morning, the village children went to
school. In the afternoon, they would play in the empty
yards, wander through the abandoned cow barns and
deserted chicken coops, climb to the empty dovecotes
or the branches of trees where no bird had a nest.

Day after day, in the evening – only if it hadn't
rained – Solina the Seamstress would take her invalid
husband for a walk through the village streets. The
invalid, Ginome, had shrunk so much over the years
that Solina could easily lay him in an old pram and
wheel him to the riverbank and back.

All the way there and back, Ginome, wrapped in nappies, would bleat in a thin, whiny voice because his amnesia made him think he was a baby goat. Solina would lean over and hum to him in her dark, warm voice: Hush, hush, hushabye, hush, hush my little Ginome, all alone, hush, hush, hushabye.

Sometimes Little Nimi, his hair tangled and filthy, his clothes torn and his nose runny, would dash past them, one eye watering. Panting, he'd wave at them from a distance and give them two or three long, wild whoops. The invalid would immediately stop bleating, smile with baby-like pleasure and turn his head to listen.

With one hand, Solina would gently stroke the sparse grey hair that still grew on her husband's head, and with the other, she kept pushing his pram, its ancient wheels squeaking along the sloping path.

In the long summer evenings, at the end of their work day, Danir the Roofer and his two helpers would sometimes sit down to rest on the low stone wall in the village square and drink beer from thick glasses, and sometimes the three of them would begin to sing. Other young men and women came from the far ends of the village to gather in the stone square and join in the singing or play games of skill or argue and whisper to each other. Occasionally, they burst out laughing. The children of the village would sneak into the square to listen or watch them from behind the fences because sometimes the young men and women would talk and joke about things that children weren't allowed to hear, for instance about other villages located in the valley far below, or about the love lives of rabbits or what the howls of cats on heat sound like. Danir the Roofer sometimes roared with deep, hoarse laughter that sounded like a cascade of rocks, and swore that soon now, in another week, another month, he'd take his helpers down to the far-off valleys and they'd come back not on foot, but in a convoy of wagons harnessed to horses and loaded with a hundred different kinds of birds, animals, fish and insects. They'd go from house to house and scatter the animals in every yard and release the fish into the waters of our river. So the village would be just the way it had been before that cursed night. The young men and women were stunned into silence by those words: instead of making them laugh, Danir's words suddenly cast a shadow over the square.

Those evening get-togethers of Danir the Roofer and his gang of friends in the square paved with ancient stone tiles were actually the only happy moments in the life of the village. Because soon after sunset, the group would disperse quickly, each to his own home. The square emptied in an instant, leaving only the shadow.

Later, when night fell, all the houses were locked up with iron bolts and the windows covered over with iron shutters. No one went out after nightfall. At ten o'clock, the lights were turned off, one by one, in the windows of the small houses. The only light filtering out came from the table lamp in Almon the Fisherman's shack at the edge of the village. But at midnight, his window too was dark.

Darkness and silence crept from the depths of the forest and lay heavily on the sealed houses and deserted gardens. Massed shadows quivered on the village paths. Cold winds sometimes blew in from the mountain, rustling treetops and bushes. The river seethed all night and rushed down the slope, foaming and bubbling through the darkness.

5

For a terrible fear filled the village at night.

Night after night, the entire outside world belonged to Nehi, the Mountain Demon. Night after night – or so the parents whispered to their children behind the closed iron shutters – Nehi the Mountain Demon comes down from his black castle beyond the ridges and forests and passes among the houses like an evil spirit, searching for signs of life. If he happens to find a stray grasshopper, a solitary firefly blown here from far away by the winter winds, or even a beetle or an ant, he whips open his dark cape and ensnares any living thing inside it, and before sunrise, he flies back to his castle of horrors beyond the most distant forests on the perpetually cloud-shrouded mountain tops.

That's what the parents whispered to their children,

18

but when the story ended, they assured them in a different voice that those were only fairy tales. Yet none of the villagers ever went out after dark. Because the dark, the parents said, the dark is full of things it is definitely better not to meet.

Maya, only daughter of Lilia the Widowed Baker, was a stubborn child. She didn't want to hear such rumours and refused to believe in things no one had ever seen. Maya was often cheeky to her mother: she said that all the darkness stories her mother read to her were silly and stupid. Sometimes Maya said, Everyone in this village is a little crazy, Mum, and you're a little crazier than any of them.

Lilia said, Maybe it's a good thing you feel that way. Maybe there really is an old craziness here in the village. And you'd be better off knowing nothing about it, Maya. Nothing. Because people who don't know can't be thought guilty. And they're not likely to catch it.

Catch what, Mum?

Bad things, Maya. Very bad things. Enough. Have you by any chance seen my kerchief anywhere, the brown one? And when will you finally stop scribbling on the oilcloth table cover? I've asked you a thousand times to stop. So stop. Enough. Finished.

One night, Maya waited patiently under her winter covers until her mother fell asleep. Then she got out of bed and stood at the window without turning on a light. She stood there at the window till morning, wrapped in her winter covers against the cold, and she didn't see anyone walk past outside, didn't hear anything, except once when she thought she heard the sound of Nimi the Owl's sad whoops coming from three streets away. Nimi had become a wandering street child and all the doors of the village were closed to him because of his whoopitis. But then he was silent. In the flawed moonlight that occasionally peeped from between the clouds, Maya saw clearly the clump of black trees across the street behind the ruins of a house.

And because the night was very long and empty, she waited for the moon to shine briefly through the clouds and counted eight trees there. An hour or two later, when the moon shone through again, she recounted them, and this time there were nine. The next time there was light, she counted again, and there were still exactly nine trees. But in the small hours of the morning when the mountain slopes began to grow pale as the first fingers of dawn touched them, Maya decided to count those trees one last time, and suddenly there were only eight again.

She got the same result when she counted them the next day, in the light, after she decided to go to the ruins and check it close up: exactly eight trees. To be on the safe side, Maya went from tree to tree, touched each trunk and counted in a whisper, twice, from one to eight. There was no ninth tree. Had she made a mistake in the middle of the night? Because she was tired? Because it was so dark?

Maya didn't say a word about the ninth tree, not to her mother, Lilia the Widowed Baker, not to her friends and not to Emanuella the Teacher. She told only Matti because Matti had told her about the secret plan he'd been working on in his mind for months. Matti listened to Maya's story about the ninth tree, thought for a while – didn't hurry to answer – and finally said that one night soon, he too would stay awake and wait patiently until his parents and sisters fell asleep, then sneak outside to the clump of trees that grew behind the ruins. He'd stand there all night, he wouldn't doze off for even a minute, wouldn't take his eyes off them, and he'd count them himself to see whether, at one of the darkest hours of the night, something else appeared there, a tree or not a tree, something that vanished a few moments before the first light of day.

6

I T ALL began many years before the children of
the village were born, in the days when even their
parents were still only children: suddenly, one wet
and stormy winter night, all the animals vanished
from the village, livestock, birds, fish, insects and
reptiles, and the next morning, only the villagers
and their children were left. Emanuella, who was
nine years old at the time, missed her tortoiseshell
cat Tima so much that she cried for weeks. Tima
had given birth to three kittens, two tortoiseshells
like her and one playful marmalade kitten who loved
to pretend he was a rolled-up sock and hide in a
boot. That terrible night, the cat and her kittens
disappeared, leaving behind an empty, lined shoe
drawer at the bottom of the wardrobe. The next
morning, all Emanuella found in that drawer was

a small ball of cat hair, two whiskers and the sweet-sour smell of warm kittens, licky tongues and milk.

There are a few old people in the village ready to swear that on that night, through cracks in the shutters, they saw the shadow of Nehi the Demon passing through the village in the dark at the head of a long, long procession of shadows. The procession was joined by all the animals from every yard, every chicken coop and pen and paddock and stable and doghouse and dovecote and cow barn, a host of silhouettes large and small, and the forest swallowed them all up. By morning, the entire village had emptied of animal life and only the villagers were left.

For many days afterwards, people were careful not to look each other in the eye. Out of suspicion. Or shock. Or shame. From that day to this, most of them have tended not to talk about all of that. Not a word, good or bad. Sometimes they even forget why. In fact, they prefer to forget. And yet they all remember quite well, silently, that they're better off not remembering. And there's a need to deny everything, to deny even the silence itself, and to ridicule those who nonetheless remember: they should keep quiet. They should not speak.

That night, Solina the Seamstress, who had once tended goats and raised chickens, lost her flock, her chicken coop and her ducks. And at dawn, her small cage of songbirds was left empty. Her husband, Ginome the Blacksmith, disappeared the next day and wasn't found until a week later, shaking and frozen with cold among the trees of the forest, perhaps because he had gathered the courage to go out and look for his herd of goats and the vanished farmyard birds. When his wife, Solina, and all the village elders asked him what he had seen, all they could get out of him were wails and sobs. That's when Ginome began to lose his memory. After that, his body began to shrink and shrivel and collapse into itself until it could fit into an old pram and he himself turned into a sort of lamb. Or kid.

Years ago, Almon the old fisherman set down a detailed description in his notebook of what happened that night. He wrote that on that last evening, right before darkness fell, when he went down to the river and took his fishing net out of the water, he found nine live fish in it. He decided to leave those fish in a tub filled with water near his front door till he took them out to sell in the

25

morning. When he woke up the next morning, there was the tub, still filled with water but empty of fish.

And the same night, Zito, Almon's faithful dog, vanished for ever too. Zito was a very feeling dog, but as logical as a clock, a quiet dog with one brown-and-white ear and one completely brown ear. When he was trying very hard to concentrate and understand what was happening in front of his nose he used to cock his ears forward so they were almost touching. When he cocked his ears this way, that dog looked serious and hugely intelligent and thoughtful, for a moment like a dedicated scientist concentrating as hard as he can, nearly, so nearly about to unlock one of science's secrets.

And sometimes Zito, Almon the Fisherman's dog, could read his master's mind. That dog could guess what his master's thoughts were even before he began thinking them: he would suddenly get up from where he was lying in front of the stove, cross the room and stand resolutely at the door less than half a minute before Almon looked at the clock and decided it was time to go out to the riverbank. Or that dog would lick Almon's cheek with his warm tongue, lick it with love and compassion to comfort

26

him when a sad thought was just about to settle in his brain.

Despite all the years that had passed since that night, the old fisherman had not been able to reconcile himself to the dog's disappearance: after all, they'd been connected to each other by a love filled with tenderness and care and trust. Was it possible that the dog had suddenly forgotten his master? Or perhaps something terrible had happened to him? For if Zito were alive, he would surely have escaped from whoever had kidnapped him and made his way home. Sometimes Almon thought that he could hear the muted echo of a thin howl calling to him from very far away, from the heart of the thick forest: Come, come to me, don't be afraid.

It was not only Zito who disappeared that night, but also a pair of small finches that used to sing to Almon the Fisherman from their nest of twigs on a branch that gently grazed his window whenever the wind blew. And the woodworms that used to fill Almon's sleep at night with the sound of their quiet gnawing as they ceaselessly dug their tunnels through his old furniture. Even those woodworms had been silenced for ever since that night.

For many years, the fisherman had been used to falling asleep every night to the gnawing sounds those woodworms made as they munched away at the innards of his furniture in the dark. That's why, since that terrible night, he hasn't been able to fall asleep: as if the depth of the silence is mocking him from the darkness. And so, night after night, Almon the Fisherman sits at his kitchen table till midnight, remembering how once, at that hour, the forlorn cry of foxes used to filter in through the closed shutters and the yard dogs would answer the forest foxes with angry barks that would end in a howl. At those times, his beloved dog used to come and rest his warm head on Almon's lap, look up at him with an expression of deep understanding, an expression that radiated a silent glow of compassion, love and sadness. Until Almon would say, Thank you, Zito. Enough. I'm almost over it now.

So Almon would sit, thinking alone in the night silence, missing his dog, missing the finches and fish and even the woodworms, and write and rub out words in his notebook, sometimes hearing from a distance the thin voice of Little Nimi as he ran alone from yard to yard in the dark, making whooping noises that sounded from afar like sobs. At those moments, Almon the Fisherman would begin to berate his pencil, argue loudly with the stove or riffle the pages of his notebook to try to block out the clamour of the night and the roar of the river.

Almon wrote in his notebook that without any living creatures, even the clearest summer nights sometimes seemed overlaid with a murky fog, a fog that descended on everything and almost buried the village, the heart and the forest under it. Summer-night-haze, Almon the Fisherman wrote in his notebook, not spongy and soft like winter-frost-vapour, but dusty, dirty and depressing.

Since that night when Nehi the Demon took away all the creatures, pulling them along behind him to a hiding place on the mountain, the villagers lived and cultivated their orchards in silence and fear. Without a single pet, without a single farm animal. Alone. Only the river still passed through the village, rolling pebbles, broken branches, clumps of mud in the foam of its flow. Day and night, winter and summer, that river never rested.

7

S OMETIMES BRAVE woodcutters and also Danir the Roofer and his young friends would venture out to the edge of the forest, but even they didn't dare to go into the forest alone, only in groups of three or four, and always in daylight.

Never, never ever under any circumstance, parents told their children, never ever ever go out of the house after nightfall. If a child asked why, his parents would glower and say, because the night is very dangerous. Darkness is a cruel enemy.

But every child knew.

Sometimes, at dawn, the woodcutters could see broken branches and trampled grass, and they would look at each and shake their heads without saying a word. They knew that after nightfall, Nehi the Mountain Demon comes down from his high mountain castle and wanders in the forests that surround the village, and at midnight his shadow glides along the river, and he touches orchard fences with his fingers, passes soundlessly among the shuttered houses, through the dark yards, sails among the abandoned stables and deserted cow barns. The grass he steps on and the leaves he brushes against tremble with the whoosh of his black cloak, and only near dawn is he swallowed up in the depths of the forest, slipping away into the tangle of trees in the dark, gliding silently among the valleys, caves and clefts, returning to his castle of horrors somewhere in the high mountains no man has ever dared to approach.

Look, the woodcutters would whisper to each other early in the morning, Look, he was right here just last night. Only five or six hours ago he passed through here without a sound, right here, where we're standing. The thought made chills run down their spines.

8

ONE NIGHT Matti decided to keep the promise he'd made to Maya. But he didn't have the courage to get dressed, sneak outside and walk to the small grove near the ruins. Instead, Matti waited patiently until his parents and sisters were asleep, got out of bed and slipped barefoot to the kitchen window that looked diagonally out on to the grove, and stood there, awake and sharp-eyed, till morning. He was able to count the silhouettes of nine trees at the foot of the ruined house. There were nine trees all night, and when the sun began to rise, there were still nine, so Matti decided that Maya must have been so frightened or jumpy that she had made a mistake. Or maybe she just fell asleep and had a dream.

But in class the next day, when he told her in a

whisper, Maya said, Come on, Matti, let's go after school and count how many trees are really there. And they went to the slope where the ruins were and counted carefully, touching each and every tree and saying its number out loud, and again there were only eight, not nine.

In class, on either side of the blackboard, between the windows and over the bookcase, Emanuella the Teacher had hung warning signs in black and red: THE FOREST IS DANGEROUS. BEWARE OF THE MOUNTAINS. EVERY BUSH COULD BE PLOTTING TO TRAP YOU. EVERY ROCK MIGHT BE HIDING SOME-THING THAT IS NOT A ROCK BEHIND IT. A CHILD WHO WANDERS DOWN TO THE VALLEYS ALONE MIGHT NEVER COME BACK, OR HE MIGHT HAVE WHOOPITIS IF HE DOES. THE DARKNESS HATES US. THE OUTDOORS IS FILLED WITH DANGERS.

From the depth of the woods, from the heart of the thick pine forests that completely surrounded the village, a hushed wind of darkness blew from morning till night. Even in the summer months, a dark wind shadow seeped into the village from the forests. And the river, frothing, bubbling, wound through the yards and rushed into the valley, white foam on its banks, as if racing as fast as it could to get far away, yet lingering there for a moment to curse the whole village.

9

MAYA AND Matti were the only children in the village to feel the pull of the dark woods. It was actually because of all the warnings and silence and fear that they were so drawn to the forest, and imagination tempted them to try to find out what was hidden in its depths. Matti also had an unfinished plan he told Maya about because he knew that Maya was braver than he. But it wasn't only the plan and the desire to go into the forest that they shared; they also had a deep dark secret they told no one, not their parents, not Emanuella the Teacher, not Matti's older sisters, not Almon or Danir the Roofer, not their friends at school. Only when there were no other ears around to hear did Maya and Matti whisper together and nurture their secret, the secret that belonged only to them. Often,

Matti and Maya would meet on the sly in the afternoon in an abandoned, dilapidated old stable in Matti's backyard out of earshot of his parents and sisters, and whisper their secret.

The village children, including Matti's older sisters, noticed those two whispering to each other, and immediately decided that Maya and Matti must be in love, perhaps even 'a couple'. And if they were 'a couple', then it was surely fair, even expected, to gossip about them a little, even to make fun of them and tease them a bit. After all, everywhere, a boy and a girl who want to be alone together from time to time, instead of always being with their friends, are always considered a couple. And couples always stir up envy. And envy hurts and swells and begins to secrete ridicule, almost the way a dirty sore leaks pus.

That wasn't how Matti and Maya saw themselves: they didn't consider themselves a couple at all, just the only ones who shared the secret. They never held hands or looked deeply into each other's eyes or exchanged private smiles, and they certainly never kissed, though both had tried to imagine, two or three times, how a kiss would feel and maybe how to make it happen.

But they never spoke about those imaginings. Not a single word. What joined Maya and Matti wasn't love, but a secret only they could ever know.

It was their secret and the way they were teased that made Maya and Matti feel so close and alone, because if others found out their secret, they would laugh at them a lot more and taunt and tease them twice as much. After all, anyone who refuses to be like the rest of us must have whoopitis or hootosis or whatever, and he shouldn't dare get close to us, he should keep his distance, please, so as not to infect us too. Some also ridiculed Almon the Fisherman for his thought-notebook, for his habit of standing at the far end of the yard every morning and evening, whistling to a dog that had most likely died years before, and for the completely unnecessary scarecrow he'd put up in the vegetable beds in his garden. They especially liked to make fun, behind his back, of the long arguments he sometimes had with himself or his scarecrow. Often, the former fisherman would argue even with the river, the moon, the passing clouds in the sky. In the village, they had a good laugh at the emotional reconciliations that took place after every argument between Almon

37

and the scarecrow or Almon and the wall and the bench.

The villagers also took great pleasure in mocking Lilia the Widowed Baker, Maya's mother, and they even made a circular motion with their finger near their forehead in her honour, come look see, here she is again, that peculiar woman who crumbles the loaves of bread she hasn't managed to sell during the day and throws the crumbs into the river or scatters them among the trees. Maybe by a miracle, a stray fish might suddenly pass through our village or a lost bird might accidentally be swept into our sky.

True, some of those who were used to making fun of Lilia's crumbs would sometimes linger for a moment or two at the foot of the trees or the bank of the river, stand there and wait: maybe just once? Despite everything? Why not? But a moment later they would rouse themselves as if someone had suddenly clapped near their ear. And they would shrug and walk away, slightly embarrassed.

But the whole village had no qualms about ridiculing, openly and with ugly laughter, poor penniless Solina the Seamstress and her invalid husband Ginome, whose memory was gone and body so

shrunken that he had become a baby as small as a
pillow, who bleated in a thin voice like a lost lamb.
Every evening, Solina, his wife, wrapped him in
nappies, covered him with two wool blankets and
took him in a pram for a long walk through the
streets of the village all the way to the banks of the
river whose angry roar made Ginome bleat in a
sharp, despairing voice, as if all were already lost.

10

A ND THIS was the secret: once, Mattie and Maya
were walking barefoot along the river to collect
round, polished pebbles that Matti's mother used
to make the small pieces of jewellery she sold. In
one of the bends of the river, in a hidden place,
some water had drained into a cranny, creating a
sort of shaded pool concealed in a block of grey
rock, a very small pool, almost as small as the space
between the legs of a chair. A tangle of water plants
hid the bottom of the pool. Those water plants scattered the sun reflected there, as if it were shattered
into slivers in the water: a host of shimmering, bright
gold sparkles were ignited in the pool.

And suddenly, between the water plants and the
sides of the rock, it can't be, darting, dazzling, flick-
ering, glistening, wriggling, but how could it be,

glittering like a knife in the water, shimmering live-silver scales dancing, was a fish, look, a fish, but how could it be a fish? It can't be a fish, are you really really sure, Maya, that you saw a fish here too? Really? Because, I, listen, I am absolutely, positively sure that, even though it's completely impossible, it's a fish. A fish, Maya, a fish, a live fish, you and I, we both just saw a fish here, and we didn't just think we saw it, we could see clearly that it was definitely a fish.

A fish and not just a leaf, a fish and not a sliver of metal, a fish, I'm telling you, Matti, a real live fish, a fish without a shadow of a doubt, a fish, I saw it, and so did you, it was a fish, a whole fish and nothing but a fish.

It was a small fish, a tiny fish, half a finger long, and it had silver scales and delicate lacy fins and pulsating transparent gills. Its round, wide-open fish eyes had looked at them both for a moment, as if it were saying to Maya and Matti that all of us, all the living creatures on this planet, people and animals, birds, insects, reptiles and fish, we're all actually very much alike, despite the many differences between us: almost all of us have eyes with which to see shapes and movement and colours, or at least feel the shifting light and darkness through our skin, and almost all of us hear sounds and echoes of sounds. And we all constantly absorb and classify smells, tastes and sensations.

And more: all of us, without exception, are sometimes frightened, even terrified, and we're all sometimes tired or hungry, and each of us is attracted to certain things and repelled by other things we think are disgusting. And all of us, without exception, are very vulnerable. All of us, people-insects-birds-fish, all of us go to sleep and wake up, go to sleep again and wake up again, all of us try hard to be comfortable, not too hot and not too cold, all of us, without exception, try most of the time to take good care of ourselves and keep away from things that cut or bite or prick. And all of us, bird and worm, cat and child and wolf, every one of us tries most of the time to avoid pain and danger as best we can, and yet we put ourselves in danger every time we go out to seek food or fun, even adventures, thrills, power or pleasure.

So much so, Maya said after turning this thought around in her mind a bit, so much so that we can actually say that all of us, without exception, are in the same boat: not only all the children, not only the whole village, not only all people, but all living things. All of us. But I'm still not sure what the right answer is to the question, are plants in some way our distant relatives?

So anyone who mocks or hurts another passenger, Matti said, is actually being stupid and hurting the whole boat. After all, no one here has another boat.

A moment later, or perhaps in less than a moment, the small fish twisted its body, spread the fan of its slender fins widely and plunged into the dark water, down to the river plants.

That was the only animal Maya and Matti had ever seen in their lives. Except for some drawings of cows-horses-dogs-birds on the pages of books or on the walls of Emanuella the Teacher's classroom, and the small carvings Almon the Fisherman made and gave to the village children.

Maya and Matti knew it was a fish because they had seen fish in picture books. And they knew without a doubt that it was a live fish and not a drawing because no creature drawn in those picture books could move its muscles, twist and turn, and slip away from them so quickly, dive so suddenly to a deep, invisible place among the shadows of the water plants.

11

T HAT WAS the first living creature seen in the village for many years, since that horrible night when Nehi the Mountain Demon gathered a long procession of animals, from horse to dove, from mouse to sheep to bull, and led them out of the village for ever. Some of the parents, without any warning, would suddenly be flooded by a wave of longing or sorrow and begin to imitate animal sounds for their children: the chirping of a bird and the lowing of a cow, the howling of a wolf in the forest, the cooing of a dove and buzzing of a bee and the flapping of a river goose's wings and the croaking of a frog and the whoop of an owl. But a moment later, those parents denied that they were sad, pretended that, in fact, they only meant to entertain their children a bit, nothing more, and insisted that none of those sounds were part of the real world, but existed only in fairy tales and legends.

The twists and turns of the villagers' memories were strange: the things they tried very hard to remember sometimes eluded them and hid deep under the blanket of forgetfulness. And the things they decided they'd be much better off forgetting were the ones that would rise out of the forgetfulness as if to deliberately upset them. There were times when they remembered the smallest detail of what had almost never been. Or they remembered what had been and no longer existed, remembered it with pain and longing, but their shame or sorrow was so great that they would decide firmly that it had all been a dream. And they would say to their children: it's just a fairy tale.

Others said: It was just a little joke. That's all.

Some children, when they heard those stories, felt a vague longing for what might have been there once, and perhaps had never been at all. But many children never wanted to hear those stories, or heard them and made fun of their parents and of Emanuella the Teacher: no animals had been seen for so many years that most of the children came to the conclusion that all those moos and coos and maas and meows, all those bzzzes and baas and yaps and quacks were all just strange inventions their parents had come up with, old-fashioned superstitions that should be tossed away so they could finally live in the real world, because people who live in their imaginations are not like the rest of us, and people who aren't like the rest of us will get whoopitis, and everyone will avoid them, and then it will be too late to save them.

Perhaps only Danir – the jolly, long-legged roofer, favourite of all the village girls, who loved to sing all day with his helpers as they worked on the high, slanted housetops, and liked to stop on his way home and talk to children through open windows as if they were grown-ups, or the opposite, to chat with them as if he himself were still a child, and also liked to whistle tunes in the streets under the windows of the village girls – perhaps Danir was the only one they should ask what was true and what wasn't.

But the trouble was that with Danir and his friends, who gathered around him in the stone square on long summer evenings, you could never ever know when they were joking or playing tricks on you or on each other. And if they did speak seriously, even then they seemed to be joking. Anyone who tried to have a real conversation with them also found himself, for some reason, suddenly speaking in jest. Even if he definitely didn't mean to.

Almon the Fisherman, who nobody listened to because everyone made fun of him, was the only one in the entire village who could teach the children that the real world is not only what the eye sees and the ear hears and the fingers touch, but also what the eye cannot see, the ear cannot hear and the fingers cannot touch. And it shows itself sometimes, for only a moment, to those who see with their mind's eye and know how to listen and hear with the ears of their soul and touch with the fingers of their mind. But who wanted to listen to Almon? He was a long-winded, almost blind old man who stood there and argued endlessly with his ugly old scarecrow.

12

AND AFTER the fish had gone, they could see the shock and fear on each other's faces: the mouth that dropped open, the eyes that gaped, the white-as-a-sheet paleness that spread over their forehead and cheeks. Tell me, Maya said, did you hear what I heard? Tell me, Matti said, did you hear it too? Had they really heard three or four muted, dream-like sounds rolling down from far, far away beyond the valleys and slopes, from the edges of the steep forests on the northern cliff of the mountain ridge, low-dark echoes that sounded like the barking of dogs, then faded quickly?

Maya and Matti had heard how dogs bark in Emanuella the Teacher's stories, but was there anyone who didn't make fun of poor Emanuella the Teacher who went after every man but, in the whole village, had never found herself even the shadow of a husband who would deign to glance in her direction?

And now, a little while after seeing the fish, Maya and Matti thought that the faint sounds coming from the northern ridge sounded a bit like barking. Or maybe it wasn't the barking of real dogs? Maybe it was just a distant rockfall? Or a trick of the tree-tops panting with excitement, beginning to screech and sigh with the onslaught of the gusting wind?

Who would believe that Maya and Matti had seen a live fish in the river? Or that, at almost the same time, they had heard the sound of dogs barking in the distance? Was there anyone who wouldn't laugh at them? Sometimes, one of the children would come to the schoolyard in the morning and try to tell the others about how he heard – he swears he heard it – a sound that might have been a chirp. Or a buzz. Not for a second did the children believe the boy who told those stories, and they made fun of him and teased him and said, you better stop it, and fast, before you end up like Nimi the Owl.

Perhaps because ridicule protects the ridiculers

from the risk of loneliness? Because they ridicule in groups, and the one they ridicule is always alone?

And the grown-ups? Perhaps only because they tried so hard to silence an inner whisper? Or were ashamed of a certain guilt they felt?

Matti and Maya went back to that place many times, bent over the pool, their faces so close to its surface that their noses almost sank into the water, but the little fish never appeared again. In vain they searched every one of the dozens or hundreds of the river's small pools scattered here and there in the banks alongside the flowing torrent, among the rocks, in hidden bays, in places where water plants concealed the golden sand of the riverbed.

But once, towards evening, it happened that something suddenly passed very very high over their heads: something glided high in the darkening sky, something sailed by, slight and illuminated like a single cloud in the evening air, back and forth from the forest, completely transparent, slowly and silently passing high over their heads, then back to the forest, and faded almost before Maya and Matti realised they were seeing it.

Almost – but not before they managed to see that

something was there and had passed over their heads, soaring and silent, floating onward, very high above the village and river, high above the dark forests. And Maya and Matti's eyes met and they both shivered.

13

S o it happened that those children, Matti and Maya, like an underground cell with only two members, began to convince each other that perhaps animals really did exist somewhere. Matti was very frightened, Maya a bit less, and yet they were still drawn, as if under a spell, to set out on a great adventure to find signs of life. The decision to plan such an adventure didn't come easily for Matti and Maya. They didn't completely trust themselves: perhaps the little fish and the barking sounds were tricks of their imagination? Perhaps it had only been a shiny silver leaf rising from the water for a moment before it sank and disappeared? Perhaps an old tree had broken in one of the distant forests and it was only the echo of the break that had been carried on the wind to them, and had sounded vaguely like barking? How and where should they begin their adventure? And what would happen if they were caught and punished? And everyone made fun of them? What if they came down with whoopitis, like Nimi the Owl?

And what would happen to them if they made Nehi the Mountain Demon angry? What if they too vanished for ever under his black cape just as all the animals had vanished so many years ago – so the grown-ups say – from the village and its surroundings?

And in fact, where should they begin their search?

14

T HE ANSWER to that question, their hearts told them, was that they should begin their search in the forest. The answer frightened Matti and Maya so much that for three or four weeks they stopped whispering to each other about the plan for their adventure. As if something so shameful had happened between them that it was better to pretend it had never happened. Or it had happened but was completely forgotten.

But the adventure had already taken root so deeply that it seeped into their dreams at night. They no longer felt happy or curious or excited or brave about it, but had only a dull, nagging feeling that this was it. That this is how it was and there was nothing they could do about it. That from now on, it was their responsibility. That, in fact, they had no choice.

So they continued to whisper together about the forest, the little fish in the pool, the distant barking of the dogs, the cloud that had passed over their heads but wasn't a cloud, and other signs of life. Again, that whispering led to all sorts of rumours, winks and chuckles among their classmates and sharp-eyed neighbours: Look at that pair, they're probably holding hands already. Hands? What hands? I bet they're kissing already. And who knows, maybe they've even let each other have a look?

Some people even said that they were actually a good match, those two oddballs, she with that mother of hers, the crazy baker who throws bread-crumbs into a river that has no fish or scatters them under trees that have no birds, and he with the things he writes in his little pads and doesn't show us, but runs straight to show them to Almon the Fisherman, who argues with the walls. Or maybe he doesn't show what he writes to Almon, only to Almon's scarecrow?

So the ridicule accumulated around them like a dark mud stain that spreads in water and makes it murky. But Matti and Maya had already dug through the ridicule and come out on the other side: one morning they got up very early and instead of going to school walked out of the village and straight up to the forest.

15

MAYA AND Matti walked up along the bank of the river, but they didn't hold hands except perhaps once or twice when they crossed the river on the slippery rocks scattered across it at one of the bends. As they jumped from one wet stone to another to reach the other side, they had to hold on to each other to keep from falling into the cold river. The higher up the mountain they climbed, the thicker the forest grew. Occasionally they had to push away branches and bushes and draw aside climbing ferns so they could make their way through.

There were moments when they felt they weren't alone in the forest, that someone else, or something else, was there, broad and large and dark, something that seemed to be breathing deeply and quietly behind them. But wherever they looked, they saw only thick, green plants that seemed to be turning blacker and blacker. And no matter how hard they strained their ears, they heard nothing but the whispering of the wind in the treetops, the churning of the river among the rocks and the crunch of dry leaves and branches under their shoes.

Every now and then the tangle of trees and bushes grew so dense that they could move forward only if they bent over or crawled on their hands and knees. From time to time, they passed the opening of a cave, but when they looked inside, they saw only black darkness crouched there and breathing at them, giving off the ancient smells of dust and thick mildew.

Then suddenly they passed a cave opening that didn't smell of mildew, but gave off the pleasant fragrance of a wood fire that sweetened the air as a gentle curl of smoke drifted out from inside. At first, they froze, but a moment later, Matti whispered to Maya: Let's get out of here fast before anyone spots us. Maya whispered back: Before we go, I want to crawl just a little further to see what's in there because I just have to. Wait here for me, Matti. Hide behind that rock and keep guard. If you see me come flying out of there, run back down the mountain too, don't hesitate and don't wait for me. Just run home as fast as you can and don't look back. I'll run as fast as I can too. But if you see that, let's say, fifteen minutes have gone by and I haven't come out, don't keep waiting for me. Run home and try to remember exactly how we got here and tell Danir the Roofer, no one else, only him. So my mother won't be alarmed.

That frightened Matti and he was going to whisper to Maya, No, it's too dangerous, there's no way of knowing what's lying in wait for us in the cave. But he held back and said nothing because he'd always known that Maya was braver than he was and he felt a bit ashamed about it, even mocked himself.

Two curves and three rock steps led Maya into a narrow alcove at the end of the low cave. The fire made nervous shadows dance on the soot-covered walls. Pleasant-smelling smoke rose from the fire. And Matti, after some hesitation, decided not to listen to Maya but to follow her into the cave: two curves and two rock steps, but before the third step, his courage ran out and he stood still,

60

hiding among the folds of the rock and peering out to see what would happen to Maya.

There was a small man sitting there alone, his back to Maya, busily tending to the fire. He probably didn't even know Maya was there, standing behind him, wary, poised to turn and run off in an instant.

The little man was prodding the fire with a stick, roasting himself some potatoes and onions, very gently rolling the roasting potatoes from side to side among the coals, kindling the embers, speaking amiably to his fire as he did so, encouraging it with kind words and congratulating himself on his success. And so he tended to his fire and spoke almost endlessly, never noticing Maya bent over, watching him from close by while Matti peeked out at them. Frightened, Matti watched Maya's back from within his rock-fold, unable to decide what he should do now. His legs begged to run away from there as fast as they could, while his feelings demanded that he go and stand next to Maya. The struggle between his legs and his feelings took so much energy that he was stuck there in the crevice between the rocks, fairly close to Maya's back but not as close as she was to the stranger, and slightly closer than she was to the opening of the cave.

Suddenly the stranger turned around and smiled easily, not the least bit surprised, as if he'd known the whole time that unexpected guests had arrived and he'd only been waiting till he could stop tending his fire for a moment to act like a proper host and welcome them:

Maya? Matti? Would you like to sit down? Rest a while? How about some roast potatoes? I also have vegetables, fruit, mushrooms and nuts. Come and sit here.

16

MATTI AND Maya were shocked to see that the man wasn't a man, but a child, and not a child they didn't know, but, of all people, Nimi, the boy everyone called Nimi the Owl, Nimi, with the constantly runny nose, who used to insist on telling everyone his dreams – shoes that turned into hedgehogs in the middle of the night, or a rubber hose that turned into a snake or an elephant's trunk – and everyone used to laugh at him. Nimi, who once went into the forest alone, where he must have come across something that frightened or shocked him so much that he came down with whoopitis. The disease had made him stop talking altogether and begin wandering around the village, whooping, his front teeth with the gap between them sticking out, one eye constantly weeping. And ever since, he'd been roaming around the village day and night, winter and summer, without a home, without a friend. Maya and Matti couldn't help him. Even his family was ashamed and gave up on him.

And here, in this cave, Matti and Maya found Nimi: not the Nimi who whooped, not the Nimi who ran away from people and climbed trees, making strange faces from up on the highest branches, but a Nimi who spoke and touched them both on the shoulder and even asked them to share his roast potatoes and onions browned in the fire. Even his weepy eye smiled at them affectionately.

Later, when the three of them sat together around the coals, full and relaxed, Nimi told them that his owl-whoops weren't a sickness at all, but a decision: he had been fed up with the taunting, the humiliation and the ridicule, and decided he would lead the life of a free child alone, without parents, neighbours, classmates, with no one to hurt his feelings, no one in the village or the whole world to tell him what to do or not to do. He decided to live all alone. To live in comfort and freedom. True, he has a too-large gap between his buck teeth, but at least he has a head behind his stupid teeth, not a poison mushroom like all those people who make fun of him. Sometimes he goes down to wander around the village yards and whoop a little, and everyone runs away from him, scared they'll catch his disease. But this is his home, this is where he lives, in this cave where he keeps all sorts of things he collects from people's backyards: books and jars, ropes and rusks, magazines, candles, fruit and vegetables, and pieces of clothing he snatches off the clothes lines. And Almon the Fisherman lets him dig for potatoes in his garden at night and pick as much fruit as he wants from the trees and gather vegetables from the garden.

How come you're not afraid of the forest? Of Nehi?

Sometimes I really am a little scared, especially at night, but not of Nehi, said Nimi. In fact, when I'm here in my cave, I'm a lot less scared than when I'm with the kids who hate me and whoop and throw stones and roof tiles at me, or when I'm with the grown-ups who point at me and say look-here-comes-that-sick-little-whooper-pity-his-poor-parents, and always warn the smaller children to keep away from me.

Tell me, Nimi, have you ever seen any living creatures here in the forest? No? What about Nehi?
Have you ever seen Nehi? And tell us something
else, is there really such a sickness as whoopitis?

Instead of answering that question, Nimi the
Owl got up, stretched, waved at them, inhaled his
snot, smiled with his crooked teeth and one weepy
eye – smiled to himself, not at Maya and Matti –
jumped between them and squeezed his way to the
opening of his cave. Then suddenly he let out a
long, trilling, ear-splitting whoop that sounded
despairing and belligerent at the same time. He
raced out of the cave into the thick trees, whooping
with joy at the top of his lungs, his voice fading
as he moved further away until it was swallowed
up in the depths of the forest.

When the fire died in Nimi's cave, Matti and
Maya decided to continue climbing the forested
mountain road that grew steeper and more tortuous,
more and more like a narrow dark tunnel in the
tangle of dense bushes.

Very soon, there were no more paths or cobwebs
of forest trails, only a dark, dense labyrinth filled
with thick plants, more black than green, that

blocked out the light. Some pricked and some burned, and some stung the skin like poisonous bites.

Matti and Maya tried hard not to get too far away from the river, but they couldn't stick too close to its twists and turns because in several places the river flowed through two sheer cliffs or was swallowed up under the ground, only to reappear in a totally unexpected place. But the sound of the river's flow helped Maya and Matti navigate their way up the mountain, as if it were an angry, noisy guide that was never silent: sometimes it ground its teeth as it ran over the pebbled riverbed; sometimes it growled faintly as it wandered among the cliff walls; and sometimes it roared wildly in foamy cascades.

After a few hours, they lost the river. They couldn't hear even a distant murmur of its flow. Instead, they began to hear other echoes from the hidden depths of the forest, squeals, sighs, splutters, as if something somewhere were inhaling, exhaling and whispering, something fairly close, and yet – invisible. And not far away, something else was stifling a cough, and yet another thing was sawing away stubbornly, or gnawing with strong teeth.

It would stop for a moment as if it had grown tired, then begin gnawing again.

Maya and Matti figured it must be evening already and they wanted to find themselves a cave where they could wait for morning to come. They thought it strange that daylight still filtered through the tree-tops. Matti stopped to take a breath of air and shake off some of the thorns and dry pine needles that were stuck in his clothes. Maya, who was almost always a few steps ahead, stopped to wait for him. She suggested that they continue up the mountain as long as there was some light. Then, because she could guess what his answer would be, she stated more than asked, You want us to go home.

In his heart, Matti did want to go home, but the suggestion to give up and go home had to come from her, not him.

So he asked her: What do you think, Maya?

And Maya said: And you?

He hesitated for a moment, then said in a gallant, firm voice: I think we should do whatever you say.

And Maya said: It's good that we ate with Nimi, around the fire, but I'm hungry again now, and a little tired.

Matti said: So we go back?

And Maya: Maybe. Yes. Okay. But not home. Let's go back to Nimi's cave and stay there till morning. Then in the morning, we'll keep climbing.

So they turned back. And this time, Matti was the one in the lead, struggling to pave a way for them through the thick vegetation. But the vegetation grew thicker and thicker. The more they propelled themselves forward like tired swimmers battling strong waves, the denser the bushes grew. Instead of going down, they found themselves still climbing the steep, forested slope. Again, it seemed to them that the day was beginning to fade and darkness was probably not far off, and they would never find Nimi's cave again.

A low, dark shadow suddenly passed over their heads in the total silence, sailed right over the treetops and almost touched them, hovering and darkening the tangle of trees and shrubs for a moment. Then a moment later, it moved away into the distance without a sound. As if for a while, a heavy black blanket had covered everything. And for a moment, their hearts filled with fear at a huge magic trick, fear of a day that wasn't day and a night that wasn't night. But neither Maya nor Matti said a word about it. They were silent and kept climbing. Till they reached a place on the mountainside where they could rest and make plans. Maya went alone to see what lay ahead because she thought she heard the whisper of the river in the distance.

There, on the mountainside, between two rocks, Matti bent to examine a small stone, a curled stone that reminded him of a picture of a snail, or maybe this was a fossilised snail. Meanwhile, Maya climbed further up the mountainside towards what seemed to be the murmur of the river. Suddenly, Matti couldn't see her any more, couldn't even hear the sound of her steps, but he was afraid to raise his voice and call her. And when Maya turned to look, she didn't see Matti either. He had vanished among the trees, and she too was afraid to call him because they both had the feeling that they mustn't shout here because they weren't really alone; someone was waiting for them in the depths of the forest. Or hovering above them. Or perhaps just standing silently, unmoving, among the shadows of the dense forest, never taking his eyes off them. Within the deep silence that lay heavily on everything, Matti suddenly thought that he wasn't the only one listening to the pounding of his heart, but whatever was standing in the shadows and watching him could hear it as well. And when he put the curled, snail-like stone down on the flat rock and looked for Maya but couldn't see her, another snail, not a fossilised one, crawled near his shoe. But by the time Matti looked back at it, the snail had vanished as if it had never been, swallowed up in a crack.

17

Afternoon some hesitation, Matti decided that he should stay and wait for Maya there, at the foot of the rock that looked a bit like a large axe, because what would happen if he went to look for her? She might come back on a different path while he was gone. And if she didn't find him there, she might start wandering around the forest looking for him and get lost among the hills, and they'd be looking for each other like that until darkness fell. So he sat leaning against the axe-rock and waited, trying to listen as hard as he could to pick up every rustle and murmur.

From so high up, the expanse of forest looked like a large, dark screen dotted with illuminated spots that were green, mottled green and grey-green and yellow-green and a green so dark it was almost black.

Matti's eyes searched the distance, far below him,
for the tiled roofs of the village, but the village had
disappeared. Matti conjured up a picture of Almon
the Fisherman's fruit trees. In his imagination, he
saw the vegetable garden clearly and even the scarecrow standing in its beds. And he could describe
to himself how the old fisherman walked slowly
past, sighing, limping his way among the beds
towards his wooden table, missing his dog Zito,
and the finches and the fish and even the woodworms that used to gnaw away at the innards of
his furniture every night. He was probably scolding
the scarecrow now or arguing with himself as he
walked. He always had the last word, muttering
some unanswerable response from under his thick
grey moustache. And there, not far from the ruins,
Emanuella the Teacher was standing alone hanging
laundry on the line in the backyard of her small
house. Matti knew from the gossip – the whole
village knew – that Emanuella the Teacher, not a
young woman, had been trying for years to win
the hearts of the men of the village, single and
married, young and not so young, but not one of
them gave her a second glance. Sometimes, Matti

73

would join those who made fun of her and called her Emanu-no-fella. But now he regretted that: her loneliness and desperation seemed almost painfully sad to him now. When he thought about the narrow street under his parents' house, Matti pictured Danir the Roofer and his two young helpers sitting astride the beam of a tiled roof, hammering away and laughing because they'd managed to match the beats of their three hammers to the rhythm of a jolly marching song.

And he pictured Solina the Seamstress stopping in the middle of her walk and bending over her invalid husband's pram, maybe to straighten his blanket or change a wet nappy, or maybe just to stroke his head covered with its sparse grey hair, while from the depths of his lost memory, Ginome bleated thinly, heartbreakingly, because he thought he was a kid and his wife was a surrogate mother sheep.

And maybe at that very moment, as he sits there imagining life in the village, Lilia the Baker, Maya's mother, is on her way from the bakery to the village's only grocery store in the square. And maybe she meets Solina there wheeling her husband in the pram. Lilia stops as she always does to exchange a few words with Solina, to tell her how hard it is to raise a stubborn child like Maya who is as cheeky as a devil, yes, but definitely not cruel. The whole problem is that my little girl has an overly strong and spirited nature. She knows everything better than I do and much better than everyone else, so everything always has to be exactly, but exactly the way she wants it. Then Lilia will probably brush off her apron, apologise – because, for no reason at all, she always lowers her eyes and says she's sorry – and she'll say goodbye to Solina and Ginome and continue on her way down the narrow street, pushing-rolling her old bread cart, whose wheels need to be oiled or maybe even replaced.

And why shouldn't I oil them for her myself? Matti thought. Who cares if people talk. Let them talk. They can make fun of us as much as they want. After all, Maya and I saw something they never even dreamed about. And when we come out of this forest, maybe we'll know something the village doesn't know . . . or has been trying very hard not to know. Or maybe the whole village knows and is just pretending, the way Little Nimi pretends to have whoopitis on purpose so he can stay free?

If only we get out of this forest in one piece. It should be night-time already and the whole world should be dark, but strangely, it doesn't come, it's holding back, as if under a spell.

And what if Maya has gone very far away?

What if she gets lost?

What if we both lose our way inside the cobweb of the dense forest?

And how long do we have, if we have any time at all, before it gets dark?

Maybe they haven't started worrying about us at home yet. But they'll start soon.

Matti sat that way for a long time, looking down at the valley from high up on the mountain, sunk in thoughts and imaginings. But he was actually trying to push away the fear that kept growing sharper every minute, creeping under his skin and making chills run down his spine: because Maya didn't come back and she didn't come back afterwards, and even after that, she still hadn't given a sign. He was getting more and more cross with her: where had she vanished to like that? Could she have gone back down to the village without him? And you know what, it would serve her right if I take off too and run back home right now before it gets dark.

Then his anger at Maya turned into cold fear as he listened to the rustling of the tall trees, the silence and the wind. He could already sense in the air the faint smell of the end of afternoon or the onset of evening, and the twilight wind began a whispered conversation with the rustle of the trees in the forest. Matti had already stood up and was planning to run home as fast as his legs could carry him when, through the whirring and whooshing of the wind in the pine needles, he thought he heard the barking of dogs again, coming from far, far away. For a moment, he also seemed to hear Maya calling faintly to him again and again all the way from the thick forests on the mountain above him: Matti, Ma-a-tti, come he-e-ere, co-o-ome Ma-a-atti, co-o-o-ome, co-o-o-ome . . .

And he didn't know which was the most terrifying choice: to ignore the cry that might be a desperate call for help, or to go bravely up into the forest towards the voice that might only be a trick to lure him into a dangerous trap, a voice that was coming not from up on the mountain, but from inside his head, born of the fear and desperation that had already begun to darken his heart and choke his breath like a foot in a heavy shoe pressing on his chest . . .

18

FINALLY MATTI decided to climb up the rocks. The trees of the forest around him became denser and darker as if they had crowded together deliberately to block his way. But again he found a kind of path or narrow trail among the tree trunks that wound its way up the mountain and led him to the steep slopes and into a tangle of black bushes. The path kept climbing up and up in sharp hairpins towards the top of the mountain till the sun sinking over the ridges began to paint the sky above the treetops the colour of an immense fire, then of wine, then of burning embers. Soon the sky and earth would be covered over with a cloudy curtain of ash.

Now he saw a stone wall with a gate made of thick tree stumps, and from inside, above the wall and the gate, a cloud illuminated by many colours rose and hovered, and many strange sounds came from it, high sharp sounds and deep faint sounds, and delicate soft sounds like snowflakes, whistling, chirping, panting, croaking sounds, grating sounds and soothing sounds, sounds Matti had never heard in his life, and yet he recalled them and knew they were the sounds of animals and birds, gentle mooing sounds and low growls and chorus after chorus of tweeting-twittering-singing voices. And among them was Maya's voice, clear and ringing with joy, What's wrong with you, Matti, don't stand outside like that, open the gate and come in too.

19

MATTI STOOD in front of the gate for a few minutes and thought about what to do. He had the strange, mysterious feeling that he'd already been here, and maybe more than once. That some time in the past, he had stood here in front of the gate exactly as he was standing here now. That more than once he hadn't been able to decide if he should run away or go inside. That he had already decided and gone inside and had seen. And now, if he tried as hard as he could, if he pushed his mind as far as it could go, he might suddenly remember everything he had forgotten. He might even remember what he didn't know and what he'd never seen before.

Matti looked and saw that the gate wasn't

completely closed, it was almost closed, and remembered without remembering that it had been like that the last time and that's how this gate has been always and for ever. A narrow crack was left between the two sides of the double gate. If he pushed hard, he still might be able to go inside and try to save Maya.

But wouldn't it be much safer to turn right around and run away? Run down the mountain as fast as he could and not stop running and not look back, run home while he still could? Run home and tell everything to his parents, to Emanuella the Teacher, to Danir the Roofer, to the village police, who would get organised and hurry up the mountain to save Maya? Because this was the castle of Nehi the terrifying mountain demon, and Maya was already lost, imprisoned within its walls, and you're all alone, you can't save her by yourself, and if you don't run away right now, you'll be lost too. Look, the sun is going down over these walls and the forested ridges, and if you don't start running home as fast as you can now, you'll be left standing here in the dark all by yourself, empty-handed, in front of the gates of Nehi the Mountain Demon's fortress, and you'll never ever go home again.

Matti turned around, ready to run down the mountain path, but Maya's voice stopped him. She came out and stood between the gates, her arms around a strange, round, grey lump that she was pressing to her chest, and said quietly, Come in, don't be afraid, Matti, come to me, come and see a miracle, follow me, Matti, don't be afraid, come and see how wonderful it is here.

20

A ND WHEN Matti walked closer to her, he saw
that what she had in her arms was a kitten:
not the picture of a kitten, not a toy, not a doll in
the shape of a kitten, but a furry creature, alive soft
sweet and shy that was looking at Matti with two
round eyes, its ears bent forward in curiosity and
its nose and whiskers trembling slightly as if it
weren't a kitten at all, but a serious furry philoso-
pher utterly focused on trying to understand who
this was that had suddenly appeared. And why?
And what had he brought with him? And especially
– what, in fact, was going on out there, in the
unknown worlds beyond the gate?

Matti was alarmed and drew back a bit because
he knew cats only from pictures and because the
kitten's body seemed to expand and shrink, expand

and empty out in a way Mattie thought was strange and almost frightening: never in his life had he seen or imagined that all animals breathe constantly, take air into their lungs and exhale it, then inhale it again, just like we do.

But Maya wouldn't let him off the hook. She took Matti's hand and ran his frightened fingers through the kitten's soft fur again and again until they got over their fear. Then his hand calmed down as it stroked and was stroked by the soft fur, and his arm calmed down, and his shoulder, then his whole body. And suddenly, the touch of the kitten's fur felt so good, and so did Maya's fingers as they drew his hand along the kitten's velvety back. As if her fingers were creating soft tremors and passing them on to him, warm, pleasant tremors that flowed from her hand to his, and through his hand, to the kitten's fur. Then the small creature's round, innocent eyes looked at him in wonder and closed. Mattie closed his eyes for a moment too and let his fingers absorb the waves of shivery vibrations that gently shook the kitten's body because it was purring quietly in pleasure now and rubbing its cheeks and forehead gently but firmly against the hand that was petting it. The kitten's eyes opened then almost closed again, only two greenish slits peered at Matti and said, Yes, that's right, keep stroking me, please, yes, we're both enjoying it, keep doing it, yes, like that, please, don't stop.

Suddenly, the kitten winked at Mattie, a quick but unmistakable wink, the wink of a secret shared only by the two of them: as if it were trying to tell Matti that it knew very well how much his fingers wanted to stroke it, and how much pleasure Matti was getting from the way it was rubbing against his palm, as it lay sandwiched between the kitten's fur and Maya's hand. He had never felt that kind of pleasure before, and it almost made him dizzy, because the tips of Maya's fingers fluttering over the back of his hand and the soft fur he was stroking back and forth sent wave after wave of warm shivers through him.

Matti's body relaxed and filled with tenderness, and as his body relaxed, so did his fear: he looked down and saw that his feet were already standing inside the walls. And he saw the inner garden and knew that now he was really inside, actually inside the fortress of Nehi the Mountain Demon. But instead of being terrified, Matti felt curious and excited. He looked up and saw the wondrous sights of the garden.

21

THE GARDEN was shaded and lovely, and illuminated not only by the rays of the setting sun but also by intense shafts of colourful, bright light shining from among the trees and bushes, the blossoming flower beds, the pools of water and the small crystal brooks that burbled here and there in the clefts of the rock and between the terraces.

Those lights, Maya whispered, don't come from hidden lamps, like you might think, and like I thought too when I first came in here. Great colonies of fireflies are projecting the wonderful glow that they create inside themselves.

The garden was filled with fruit trees and ornamental trees and plants and meadows. At the base of the trees, beds of ferns and flowers bloomed in a delicate array of orange and gold and purple and red and lime and yellow and turquoise and pink and crimson and violet.

Matti looked up at the dense treetops and, for the first time in his life, saw and heard a multitude of birds singing and chattering loudly and interrupting each other, suddenly spreading their wings to fly off from one branch to another. Water birds stood peacefully on the banks of the brooks, even in the middle of puddles, one foot in the water, the other folded under them, sometimes even submerging their pink beaks. Matti was flooded with a soft, deep sense of serenity he had never felt before, except perhaps in the vague, veiled memory that lies beneath all memory, the serenity of a clean and fed baby as its eyes close and it is enveloped in sweetness, falling asleep in its mother's arms as she hums a lullaby in her warm voice.

Have I really been here before? Right after I was born? Or maybe even before?

The garden was deep and broad and spread out as far as the eye could see, all the way to the flowering lower edges of the slopes that bordered on dark groves, orchards and vegetable beds. Here and there, small brooks flowed like silver-thread embroidery. And over it all, hosts of small insects and bugs hissed and whizzed and whined, their flight creating wave after wave of riotous buzzing and whirring and whooshing and zooming, as if they were working away at their job of stretching a finely woven web of thinnest metal over the entire garden, and all those delicately stretched, invisible threads were gently flitting and flapping and humming and thrumming with every gust of wind.

Strange snakes, slithering swift snakes with many legs, rustled at the bottom of the bushes. And large, lazy lizards dozed with open eyes. On the meadows and lawns of the garden, white sheep wandered and grazed, and giraffes and antelope and deer and hares roved about. And between them, like groups of holidaymakers leisurely touring a peaceful resort, packs of idle wolves, a bear or two and a pair of thick-tailed foxes wandered here and there, and one unkempt jackal came up to Maya and Matti and showed them a very long, very red tongue that seemed to pour out of the side of its mouth from between two rows of sharp, glittering teeth. The jackal suddenly began to rub its pointy head on Matti's knees, once, then again, and between each rub, looked up at them with its sad yellow eyes, a heartbreaking, pleading look, until Maya finally understood and bent down to pet its head and even tickle it a little under the chin and behind the ears, and her hand slid down its back several times, from its head to the base of its tail.

Then Maya and Matti passed four or five tired tigers lying stretched out on the meadow slope and staring, motionless, into the depths of the peaceful evening, heads resting on front paws. For a moment, those sleepy tigers reminded Matti of old Almon the Fisherman when his weary` head drops to rest on his arm flung across the pages of his notebook, nodding off in the early evening as he sits alone at his wooden table at the bottom of his garden. Matti was momentarily filled with a sense of bitter longing, a sudden desire to sit on Almon's bench and tell him about all this, to describe every detail to him, or even better – to bring Almon up here so he could see it all with his own eyes. So he could feel it with his old fingers. And to bring Solina and her baby-husband too. And Danir the Roofer along with his two helpers. And Nimi. To show this to all of them, to the whole village, to his parents, his big sisters,

Emanuella the Teacher, and to look closely at their faces when they saw the garden for the first time.

Just then a cow came towards them, a slow cow, an extremely proud and well-connected cow, a very distinguished cow adorned with black and white spots. She trudged and swayed her way slowly, filled with self-importance, past the sleepy tigers, nodding her head two or three times as if she were totally and completely and entirely not surprised, absolutely not surprised, on the contrary, all her calculations had been correct and all her early assumptions had proved to be accurate, and now she nodded also because she was pleased she was right and also because she definitely agreed with herself fully and utterly and always, and without the slightest shadow of a doubt.

22

MATTI AND Maya stared wide-eyed at all those wonders, mesmerised by the alligators with their chequered armour lying on the edge of the pool, and the monkeys, the squirrels, the parrots that circled above them in the branches of the trees that were pleasing to the eye and those that were good for food. The flapping of the sparrows' wings and the cooing of the pigeons spread a translucent veil of loveliness over the entire garden, the brooks, the meadows, the treetops, enveloping it all in a blanket of deep, warm tranquillity, the tranquillity of other worlds.

Why am I suddenly so sure that I was here once? And how can this really be?

The evening falling on that garden of wonders was so perfect, so limpid and peaceful that Maya and Matti never even noticed the not very young, not very tall man with the slightly bent back and bare head, his suntanned face grooved with a strange and intricate criss-cross of wrinkles, his long, almost completely grey hair falling to his shoulders. He was standing there quietly, leaning against a rough tree trunk, alone on the garden slope in the evening breeze, looking at them with a slight smile, a bitter, distracted smile, as if some of his thoughts were here and some were in other places.

The man's shoulders were a bit hunched, one slightly lower than the other, and his bulky hands hung limply at his sides as if they had just completed a long, very gruelling job. His face wasn't handsome, but reticent and cautious, and he looked embarrassed, as if he were glad that Matti and Maya didn't see him.

As if he felt ashamed in front of them.

And so the stranger stood there without moving, breathing slowly and deeply, and watched the fascinated eyes of the two children, followed every movement of their curious gaze as it roamed around the sights of the garden, astonished at everything in it.

The man's secretive, almost sly smile actually began around his eyes and not on his lips, and spread from there along the grooves of his wrinkles, gradually lighting up all the furrows and folds of his face from within.

And still he didn't move or make a sound. Only one bluish vein, thin and remarkably delicate, pulsed on one side of his forehead like a tiny fish twitching underwater.

Until Maya suddenly saw him and was terribly startled. But she stayed calm and simply bent over slightly and whispered to Matti, Careful, Matti, don't look over there now because someone is standing there and watching us, but he doesn't seem dangerous, just a little strange.

23

A LITTLE strange, the man with the suspicious smile repeated the words Maya had whispered to Matti. That's exactly what people said about me many years ago, when I was still just a child: he's a little strange, they used to say, and twist their lips into a sneer. And sometimes they would say, look, here comes the retard. All that was many years before you were born, when your parents were about your age.

And I wanted so much to be one of them: I really, really tried all the time to be like everyone else. Even more like them than they were. But the harder I tried, the more they made fun of me.

The stranger began to walk towards them, but after a few steps, he stopped, changed his mind and went back to the fig tree: perhaps he was afraid he

might scare them off. Or perhaps he found it difficult to move closer to them. But when he saw that
the children didn't run away from him but kept
standing where they were and looking at him, merely
moving closer together to close the space between
them, he looked down at the grass and said in a
smiling voice, I'm glad you came.

Then added, Look, I have some pomegranate
juice here. And snow water. Want some?

Matti whispered, Careful, Maya. Don't even
touch that wooden cup. You never know. Maybe
it's dangerous to drink it.

But Maya mixed some pomegranate juice with
snow water in the hollow wooden cup, drank,
laughed, wiped her mouth with the back of her
hand, and said to the man, I'm Maya. And this is
Matti. Matti's afraid you're a sorcerer. Are you a
sorcerer?

And then she said, Drink some too, Matti. Come
on, taste it. It's cold and delicious. You won't get
whoopitis from it, don't be scared. Look, none of
the animals here are afraid of this man.

Matti didn't say a word, just grabbed Maya's arm
and tried to pull her back. But Maya absolutely

refused to be pulled back, and jerked her arm out of Matti's grasp. And she didn't say a word either.

Suddenly, some peculiar, low sounds came out of the stranger's mouth, twisting sounds that weren't like words, and when he uttered them, an entire flock of excited, twittering honey-suckers, gold and turquoise and blue-spotted, landed on his shoulders and his head, and also on the children's heads and shoulders.

When the man and his guests were surrounded by the birds, he told them how, many years ago, when he was still a child, the other children had always snubbed him. After all, every class or group has one like that, the man said, unwanted, different, and wherever groups of children go, he always insists on trailing after them, and he always drags his feet a few steps behind everyone, self-conscious and shy, but ignoring the insults and ridicule, desperate to be accepted, to belong. That's why he's ready to do anything, ready to be their servant, at their beck and call, ready to play the fool to make them laugh, to volunteer to be the jester, and they can ridicule him as much as they want, even abuse him a little, he doesn't care, look, he's handing them his whole, rejected heart free of charge.

But the group just isn't interested in having him around. And not for any special reason: they absolutely don't want him and that's that. And he should get out of their sight as fast as he can. Because he's not like us and doesn't fit in. So he should go away because really, but really, no one needs him here.

Maya said, We have a boy like that too: Nimi. Nimi the Owl.

And Matti said, No. Nimi is something different. Nimi just has whoopitis. Everyone keeps away from him because it really is dangerous to get close to someone with whoopitis.

Then he leaned over to Maya and added in a whisper, It'll be dark soon, Maya, we have to try to escape right away.

Maya said, Escape? But the gate's open and no one is keeping us here. You can leave, if you're in such a hurry. But I'm staying. There's still so much to see.

And the man said, Sit down now, both of you, here, on this stone. Have a little pomegranate or fig juice with snow water. And don't worry, Matti, about the coming darkness. It'll be a bit late tonight, so we can continue talking. Just don't be afraid of this mole. He gets insulted when people are afraid of him. He's very, very old, and almost deaf, but he took the trouble to come out of his burrow just to sniff you. Sit quietly for a minute and please let him sniff. Look at how amazingly delicate his ears and paws are, and how his pink nose is quivering so gently in your honour, like the rapid beating of an excited heart. Your smell must be stirring memories from the time before his parents were born.

Matti looked from the old mole to the man, then back at the mole, and, once again, a vague remembrance passed through his mind, I've been here before, all this happened to me once, I was here and forgot everything, and even now, I still can't remember what actually happened. But I definitely remember that I forgot. I think this man must be a little lonely. Or maybe he just seems that way to me? Is he setting a trap for us? Because, from up close, Matti thought he'd seen a spark of slyness, the glimmer of a secret scheme flash across the man's wrinkled face. And when did he see it? At the moment when the man laughed and said that the darkness would be late in coming tonight, so we can all continue talking.

What if he was planning to imprison them here? For ever?

The man's veiny fingers suddenly looked to Matti like stubborn roots that clutch and entwine and never let go.

And what if this sorcerer is actually plotting to hold us here so he can take revenge against our parents and the whole village? Or not only hold us, but cast a spell on us and turn us into animals?

Matti said, It'll be dark soon. I want to go home now.

And Maya said, But I don't. I want to hear more. And I want to see more.

24

THEN THE man told them that when he was about ten and a half, he gave up on being friends with children his own age or adults and began spending his days with cats and dogs until he learned to understand and even to speak dog-words and cat-talk, not to mention horse-lingo.

After about two or three weeks, the whole village decided that the poor boy had come down with whoop-itis, and everyone was very careful not to get close to him. Finally, things became so unpleasant that even his parents gave up on him: they were shamed by the whole village and they were ashamed of him, and also made sure that his younger brothers and sisters didn't get too close to him and catch his disease.

And so, in the end, his parents and all the grown-ups let him wander around the forest alone, as free as the wind and the water, both day and night. *Eeorrrriarrr*, the man said suddenly in a different voice, and in a moment, a bear with thick, tangled brown fur came out of the bushes, rubbed its heavy head against the man's hand, looked at Matti and Maya with damp beary eyes that were full of curiosity, affection, friendship, shy modesty and a slight sense of wonder, as if those eyes wanted to explain and say, Sorry, don't be angry, I just don't understand what all this is, I'm very sad to say that I don't understand anything, forgive me, don't expect anything from me; after all, I'm just a bear.

Then the bear turned over and lay down clumsily on its broad back, its legs waving in the air, and began to rub its fur on the carpet of grass and make all sorts of humming sounds in a dark-brown bass voice, a deep but warm wintry voice. Matti quickly retreated three or four steps and tried to pull Maya by the arm, but Maya jerked her arm out of his grasp this time too: Enough, let me go! Matti, run home if that's what you want, no one is forcing you to stay. But I for one want to get to know this place.

And the man said, You're Maya. You're Matti.

I'll introduce myself too: I'm Nehi. I'm the Mountain Demon. The sorcerer. And now, meet Shigi. You don't have to be afraid of Shigi. He's a slightly childish bear, a bear that suddenly starts to dance in the middle of a rainstorm, or tries to swat flies with his too-short tail, or hides for hours among the river plants and splashes all the animals that pass by. Shigi. Stop interrupting. I'm in the middle of a story here.

As time went on, the man continued his story, I also learned the language of pigeons, crickets, frogs, goats, fish, and bees. And a few months later, after I disappeared and went off all by myself to live the life of a mountain boy in the forest, I tried to learn more and more animal languages. It wasn't hard because the languages of animals and birds have many fewer words than the languages of people, and they have only the present tense, there's no past or future at all, and they have only verbs, nouns and interjections, no other forms.

With the years, I realised that animals sometimes lie too, to escape danger or show off, or to mislead their prey, or to frighten others, and sometimes just to charm when they're courting. Like we all do.

Creatures even have special words that express joy, excitement, amazement and pleasure. And the creatures that are considered mute, like for instance butterflies, fireflies, fish, snails – even they have certain words that aren't spoken out loud but are conveyed by all sorts of small vibrations that reach the listener only through the skin, fur or feathers, not through the ears. Those vibrations are like the gentle ripples made by a leaf that falls on to the smooth surface of a lake when the water is very calm and still.

Other creatures even have certain words that resemble prayer: special words of thanks for the sunlight, and other words of thanks for gusting wind, for rain, soil, plants, light, warmth, food, smells and water. And they have words of longing. But none of the creatures' languages have any words meant to humiliate or ridicule. No, not that.

If you'd like, Maya and Matti, the man said and gently laid his heavy, tired hands on the back of a small goat that had come and curled up to rest in Shigi's brown fur, If you'd like, we'll try to teach them to you too, slowly. The way we taught Nimi, who found his way to us before you. Yes, Nimi the

Owl, Nimi with the constantly runny nose, the one everyone down below says has whoopitis. But deep in your hearts, Maya and Matti, you have both known for a long time that there is no such illness in the world. Whoopitis was invented only to keep people from getting close. To isolate people. And in fact, from now on, you two will be our guests, mine and all the creatures that live with me here in the garden of our mountain home.

Because you're staying here. With us.

The man was silent for a moment, then in a different voice, said with a kind of firm quietness that left no room for refusal or argument: Now follow me.

And he didn't wait to see whether they would come or not, but turned around and began walking serenely towards the house, and he didn't look back, but kept talking to them from where he'd left off. He told them that many years ago, he had loved a girl in his class, Emanuella, but he never told her he loved her, so it was unrequited love. Nor did he tell anyone else about his secret love, because he was afraid that everyone, and especially Emanuella herself, would insult and ridicule

106

and humiliate him twice as much if they found out.

When Matti and Maya and Shigi the bear and the little goat Sisa followed the man into the house, the children saw that it wasn't a castle at all, just one large, high-ceilinged room, a warm room built entirely of unpolished wooden beams and furnished only with simple and essential furniture, pieces sawed from tree trunks and strong branches still covered in their rough bark.

The man sat Maya and Matti down on either side of a solid and slightly clumsy table made of thick planks of wood, and the bear and the goat curled up together and fell asleep under it. Then he continued his story: One rainy, foggy winter night, he got up and ran away from the village and his home. At first, he hid in the forests, and then found himself a place here on the mountain, among the animals that all loved him and helped him and took care of him, because down below, people hurt animals too. Sometimes they even abused them.

And so, on that other rainy, foggy night, we all climbed up the mountain forest in a long procession, the man said, because the animals decided to come and live here with me. Now come to the window and get to know the place where you'll be staying from now on: all sorts of exotic fruit grow here, and the clear snow water flows in that brook with the sound of a mountain flute. See the small pool over there? In a little while, you can both take your clothes off and swim in it. Don't be shy with each other. Here, there is no shame in being naked: we are always naked under our clothes, but from the time we're little, we're taught to be ashamed of the truth and take pride in lies. And they train us not to be happy about what we have, but only about what we have that others don't. And even worse, they teach us from the moment we're born to believe all sorts of poisonous ideas that always begin with the words, 'After all, everyone . . .'

The man smiled sadly to himself and thought about that for a little while.

But here, he went on, the only shameful thing is ridicule.

And suddenly he added in a different, darker, hushed voice: And yet it sometimes happens, it happens to me almost every night, that I wake up and go down below to take revenge on them in the dark. To terrify them all to death. To glitter suddenly like a skeleton in their window panes after they've turned off the lights. Or scrape across the floors and shake the roof beams to give them nightmares. Or to wake them soaked in cold sweat, thinking they have whoopitis too. And once every few years, I draw children to me here. Like Nimi the Owl. Or you.

25

Maya hesitated a moment before she asked her questions, cautiously: But why did you actually decide to run away? Why didn't you ever try to find yourself at least one friend or two? Or a girlfriend? How come you didn't think you should at least try to change something? Or change yourself? You were never curious enough to try and figure out what exactly it was about you that made others mock you? Why you? Too many questions? No? My mother gets cross with me all the time, why do you always ask so many questions, stop it, every one of your questions puts another crack in the walls of our house.

The man didn't look at Maya or Matti, and he took his time in answering too, glancing bitterly at the tips of his fingers, at his large, dark nails. Then

he answered all of Maya's questions with five words:
It was hard for me.

A moment later, he added, I used to ask questions all the time too. But the questions just made
them mock me even more. Until there were so many
cracks that I didn't have a house left.

Matti said, Maya. Enough.

But Maya answered him angrily, Why, Matti?
Why is it enough? He's so full of self-pity that he's
completely forgetting that he himself caused the
disaster in our village. Even now, after so many
years, when you ask him why he ran away, he avoids
giving an answer.

Matti said, But Nimi ran away too. And so did
the animals themselves. But you know how it is
when the abuse starts. And the mockery. Sometimes
I think about running away from them too, from
everyone, from home, my parents, the other children, the grown-ups, my sisters, everyone, and let
them think I have whoopitis. To run away and live
all by myself in a cave in the forest so no one can
tell me do this and don't do that, and aren't you
ashamed of yourself.

Maya's answer to this was, But when you dream

about running away, Matti, you don't think about taking with you everything that grows. Or the water. Or the light. And you don't dream about how to come back at night and take revenge on everyone.

There was silence. Until Nehi said, But in fact, you both ran away too. And now the whole village is frantic because of you, and your parents are shattered and in despair.

26

A<small>ND SO</small> the two children sat in the home of Nehi the Mountain Demon all evening. And the evening went on and on as if it were under a spell, and for hours the soft evening light caressed them. After the evening light came the twilight, and after an immeasurable time, the dusk of sunset began, and that dusk went on and on and never ended, but flickered and painted the vast sky in a rainbow of gentle hues, as if up here even time itself had been erased. Wiped away. For ever.

The inside of the house confirmed what the children had seen from the outside, that it was not a fortress, only a low, wide building made of thick logs, entirely surrounded by a garden. Matti and Maya strolled through the garden and went back into the house and ate and drank and talked.

That was because, right after Nehi frightened them, he tried to make up for it by being nice to them, by offering them luscious fruit to eat, the likes of which they had never tasted before. Then they went out to the garden again to be with the animals, birds, insects, and reptiles. The light faded slowly, but darkness held back. The evening itself came and went, drifting slowly from one flower bed to the other along the garden paths, a hesitant kind of evening that didn't want to be and didn't want to cease.

It was neither day nor night.

And Matti thought, I don't remember but I haven't completely forgotten that I was here once at a time that was a little like this, a time that wasn't day and wasn't night, not light but not not-light, and in fact, there was no time, but the opposite of time, and all around me was tenderness and caring. A dream? In an illness? When I was little? In the delirium of a high fever? When I was still nursing? Or even earlier, before I was born?

Nehi, when he was still the child called Na'aman, always took pity on animals and made sure to feed them, even the flies and the ants and the fish in the river, when he was only four or five years old.

And in the village, they made fun of you for that too, Maya said.

She didn't say the words as a question, but as something she knew.

And Matti said, They still haven't forgotten that, but they don't remember it either. Maybe there should be another word, a special word that includes both remembering and forgetting: sometimes, out of the blue, a mother or father in the village imitates animal or bird sounds for their child. But a minute later, they regret it and correct themselves and explain that animals are merely a fairy tale. Then they sigh because our teacher, Emanuella, confuses us so much with all those crazy animal stories out of her poor head.

When Matti said there should be a word that would mean both remembering and forgetting, Maya thought about her mother, Lilia, who scatters breadcrumbs at the end of the day for birds that aren't there and tosses slices of bread into the river for fish that vanished a long time ago. The day was approaching its end. And right now, her mother was standing alone on the river-bank and soon they'll start to be very worried about us. Or maybe there, down below, many days and nights, sunrises and sunsets have passed, and everyone has already given up on us, and it's only here that time has stopped? And the river itself, Maya thought, that river never rests, day in and day out it churns, twisting among the yards in the village, racing stubbornly onward to the valley, rushing bubbling down the slope, white foam on its banks, as if running away from us, downward to some peaceful valley, and stops in our village for a moment only to curse it.

Maya said, We'll have to go back soon. They'll be worried about us there. They'll think something terrible has happened.

Matti said, Just a little while longer. Till the end of his story.

And the man suggested, We'll ask the darkness to hold off a while longer. We agreed with the evening a long time ago that it would approach slowly.

27

MAYA SAID, But you did a terrible thing to us by taking all the animals away. And you took animals that no one was ever cruel to. You even took animals that were loved, that were happy to be part of the family, like Almon's dog, for instance, and Emanuella's cat and her three kittens. In my opinion, kidnapping the animals was even crueller than the ridicule you suffered. And you, when you decided to take revenge, did you stop for even a minute to ask who you were really taking revenge on? The ones who made fun of you? The ones who abused their animals? Or were you taking revenge on Almon and Solina and my mother and Emanuella, who you still say you loved?

Na'aman raised his shoulders and seemed to be trying to bury his neck and head between them.

As if he had suddenly become ugly right in front of their eyes. And his hands began to dart about, searching for something, as if begging to be released from being hands, to be hidden, to be free to escape from their owner and never come back. And when Maya mentioned Emanuella's name, there suddenly appeared at the corners of Nehi's mouth a sort of grin that looked both forlorn and slightly malicious, a twitch of meanness that at the same time begged for a bit of sympathy.

What, you don't like it here? he said, suddenly hurt. You don't want to stay? Just a little longer? Okay. Go. I don't care. Go. After all, I'm not alone here. Go. I'll hold back the darkness so it doesn't overtake you before you reach home. Go. It doesn't matter. Go. If I really wanted revenge, I could keep you here with me for ever. Or at least I could counter your questions with a few difficult ones of my own. Why, for example, do all of you let your parents shut you up every time you try to find out what really happened before you were born? Why do you always let them change the subject and talk about other things? Maybe it's because you didn't really want to find out, to know? Maybe you were even afraid to know? Because it's easier to be lied to and not have the burden of all your parents' secrets placed on your young shoulders? Not just the two of you, but all the children of the village? How convenient it was for you to have your parents keep their shame and guilt to themselves and not taint you as well. Isn't that so? Or maybe you even guessed what the truth was, but your guess frightened you too much. Because if your guess was correct, then suddenly, from this day on, no one will be allowed to hurt or ridicule anyone else. And how would we live and amuse ourselves without occasionally humiliating someone? Without a touch of abuse, without mockery, without occasionally stepping on someone else?

Maya said, Look, Nehi, you yourself are mocking the rest of us now. And you're rather enjoying it, aren't you?

28

N A'AMAN WAS so lonely that he learned to speak to animals in their own tongues. Several years later, when the entire village began saying he had whoopitis and kept their distance from him and threw stones and pieces of roof tiles at him from further off, he found himself a cave in the mountains and lived there alone, surviving on mushrooms and berries. Only sometimes, at night, he would wait till all the villagers were safely shut up in their houses, then he would go down to drift like a shadow through the narrow streets of the dark village.

To this day, he still goes down there. In the dark. Goes down only when everyone is behind their iron shutters and iron bolts. Goes down to roam the village because he's sad up here, despite his love for the creatures, despite all the wonders of the mountain.

In the dark of the moonless night, he wanders through the empty, narrow streets. And sometimes, he and Nimi tiptoe around together, approaching one house or another, peeping between the slats of the shutters to watch families quietly immersed in their last, peaceful preparations for sleep.

Because it's pleasant to listen through the curtains to the bedtime story a father is reading to his daughter, or to a mother sitting on the corner of her little son's bed humming a lullaby that brings a sudden ache to Nehi's old heart. And sometimes he likes listening through a half-closed window to the sleepy bedtime conversations between tired couples as they drink their nightly tea in the warmth of their room. Or when they sit and read in the silence of the night or when the people living in one of the houses occasionally exchange a few words that break Nehi's heart and bring tears to Nimi's eyes, simple words like: You know, you look really lovely in that flowered robe. Or: I'm so glad you finally went down and fixed the cellar steps today, thank you. Or: That bedtime story you told the boy tonight was beautiful and it reminded me of my childhood.

So he wanders among the deserted yards at night

for two or three hours, alone, and sometimes with Nimi, until the last light in the village is turned off in Almon's window. Because I'm jealous. Jealous of them because of all the things they have that I never had and never will have.

Maya said, It seems that things can be pretty sad up here too.

29

B UT YOU see, I didn't take the animals, Nehi said. Certainly not all of them. One night, they all simply got up and left the village and followed me to the highest mountain forests. Even animals that loved their homes and couldn't decide whether to stay or go – like Zito, Almon the Fisherman's dog, and Emanuella's tortoiseshell cat and her kittens – even they decided in the end to go up with me, together with all the others. Not because I cast a spell on them and not because I wanted to take revenge, but because even animals have the fear that you know so well, the fear of not being like everyone else, of staying behind when everyone is going, or going when everyone is staying. None of them wants to be without its flock or be thrown out of the herd. You edge a little bit away from the swarm just once or twice, and they won't let you back in. Because you already have whoopitis.

At first, Na'aman built himself a small shack from branches in a forest clearing on the mountain top, and every day, his friends, the animals, supplied him with everything he needed: the sheep and goats let him milk them, the chickens gave him eggs, the bees made honey, the river brought him snow water, the squirrels gathered fruit and berries for him and the little moles dug up potatoes. Long, long processions of ants even carried grains of wheat from the fields in the valley so he could bake himself some bread. The wolves and the bears watched over and protected him. And so he lived for years and years, far from all humans and surrounded by the love of live creatures, big and small. The frogs shortened his name from Na'aman to Na'ai, and in the accent of the jackals and night birds, Na'ai became Nehi.

30

MANY YEARS ago, on one of his trips into the wilderness, Nehi came to a hidden valley behind seven mountain ridges and beyond seven deep ravines and found a small bush that had white and purple fruit growing on it that tasted almost exactly like meat. Nehi called them beefberries. He planted the seeds of the beefberry bush all over the forest and cultivated them till they multiplied and spread, because he discovered that all the predators liked the taste of the beefberry and ate so heartily that they had no need to prey on weaker creatures. So Nehi was able slowly to train the tiger to play with baby goats, and the wolf to watch over the flocks of sheep and even go to sleep among them so the sheep's soft wool could warm their bodies on cold nights. Creatures no longer preyed on each other in those forests, and no animal was ever afraid of predators. But they didn't forget completely.

31

A ND AFTER another stroll around the garden,
Maya and Matti already knew how to utter
a few words in sparrow-song and a sentence or two
in cat-talk and in cow-lowing, and they understood
a breath here and a flutter there of the language of
flies. Nehi and all the creatures in the garden begged
Mattie and Maya to stay there with them for at
least a few weeks.

But Matti took Maya's hand and said, They're
worried about us down there. We shouldn't distress
them so much.

Then Matti also remembered that right now, at
this very moment, just as darkness fell, all the houses
in the village were being sealed, all the shutters were
being closed and every door was being locked with
two or three iron bolts. Their parents must be so

worried about them, and maybe the whole village had gone out to look for them with torches and maybe they'd already given up searching and were in their houses now, each family behind its bars and iron shutters.

So Maya and Matti asked Nehi to send a swift deer with them, or a dog, to show them the way home down the mountain. Of course, they promised never ever to tell anyone about what they'd seen with their own eyes or what they'd heard with their own ears in the Mountain Demon's hiding place, and never to say a single word about all the magic they'd seen in his garden.

But Nehi once again gave them a pensive smile, a modest, almost shy, even sad smile, but a tiny bit sly, a smile that didn't begin on his lips, but in the wrinkles around his eyes and spread down through the network of furrows in his cheeks till it stopped and lingered briefly at the corners of his mouth. And after his smile, he said that he needed no such promises: after all, even if they did tell it all down there, even if they piled up detail upon detail upon detail, who would ever believe them? All the villagers would only laugh at them and ridicule them if they told what they had seen: the punishment of doubters is to always cast doubt, even on the doubt they themselves cast. And the punishment of the suspicious is to suspect everyone all the time. To suspect even themselves and their own suspicions.

Matti said, The minute Emanuella the Teacher or Almon the Fisherman start telling us animal stories, everyone makes fun of them. Grown-ups and children. But, sometimes, a grown-up forgets to mock for a minute, maybe he suddenly feels regret or longing, and starts talking about all the things he's going to deny completely in another minute. There's always one who starts, and all the others shut him up. But every time, it's someone else who starts. And sometimes, before class, one boy or another will tell everyone that, very early in the morning, when he was still half awake and half asleep, he thinks he heard a cheep in the distance, or a buzz or a chirp. Everyone shuts him up quickly, tells him not to talk and not to make them angry. Do the parents deny everything because they're so ashamed? Or maybe they decided not to talk so they could put an end to the sorrow. But I don't think anyone really forgot what it was the whole village decided to forget.

Then Nehi asked them to tell him a little about life in the village during the daytime. Because he goes down there only at night. He asked them to please tell him what the stone square is like during the long summer evenings between the light of day and the light of sunset. And what it's like when Danir the Roofer and his helpers and other young men and women come there to talk, drink beer, laugh and sometimes even sing for thirty minutes or an hour. And how is Almon the Fisherman? Does he still argue with the trees in his garden? Still carve wooden creatures with his penknife? One day I almost couldn't control myself or wait till midnight, that's how much I wanted to go down to his vegetable garden in the daylight, to take down the scarecrow and stand there in its place with my arms spread like a cross. Almon's almost blind, maybe he wouldn't notice the difference and then he and I could argue.

And how are the ladies' conversations in the grocery store? And the council of women who do their washing at a bend in the river? And how is Emanuella now? And the old men who come to the riverbank at ten in the morning to sit together on

benches and smoke their pipes? If I weren't afraid
that everyone would run away from me screaming
in terror, I might still go down there once in the
daytime. Just once. Slip over and sit with them,
take part in their arguments-memories and inhale
the aroma of pipe smoke. Maybe some of them
haven't completely forgotten me?

Maya said, The ones who remember are ridiculed.
The silent ones stay silent.

32

JUST IMAGINE, Maya said to Matti, and to Nehi, who was walking down the winding forest trail with them as they made their way home in the last light of dusk, just imagine what would happen if one day you finally did come home to the village, Nehi, and all the animals that left us so many years ago to go up the mountain with you came back to us too. Just imagine the panic and the shock, but think of the joy!

Matti said, And the sparrows and finches would nest in the trees again, pigeons would fly around all the dovecotes, crows would shriek at dawn, all the old cow barns and chicken coops and stables and paddocks and sheep pens would be fixed, and dogs would bark again in our yards and on the dirt roads, and swarms of bees would buzz around their hives.

Maya said, And old Almon could sit on the river-bank with his beloved dog and talk to the fish that would come back to the river, and even his old scarecrow would finally start arguing with real birds instead of with Almon.

Matti said, And Solina the Seamtress could give Ginome, her husband, a kitten of his own as a gift. Or maybe it should be a lamb. Or a squirrel.

Maya said, My mother could stroll around the village streets surrounded by a cloud of birds and scatter breadcrumbs for all of them, and Emanuella would wave hello to her from her balcony and maybe, if you came back too, Nehi, maybe, who knows –

Nehi listened in silence to everything they said. A bluish vein or artery pulsed on one side of his forehead as if the heart of a chick were beating rapidly there. But at the end of his silence, he said in his low voice, a voice as pleasant as a warm kitchen on a winter night: And what if they ridicule me again? Or abuse me? What'll happen when I suddenly have the urge to take revenge by hurting someone or I do something bad?

A moment later he added, And what if the big

brutish farmers, the ones whose parents were in my class when Rafaela, Emanuella's mother, was our teacher, what if they start beating and cursing dogs again and lash the alley cats with leather whips and poison them, and drown mice in barrels of sewage, and start going out to the forest with their rifles again to kill deer, foxes and wild goats, and sell their fur and set traps for rabbits and wild geese? And spread nets again to catch fish in the river?

When they'd gone past another five or six bends down the mountain trail that was growing dark under the thick forest treetops, Na'aman said, Of course, they'll all be happy and excited to get the cows and horses back, and the chickens that lay eggs for them and the goats and ducks and sheep and pigeons, yes, and some of them will probably get very attached to their dogs and cats and song-birds again. That – yes. But what about the rats? The worms? What'll happen to the roaches and mosquitoes and house spiders? And what'll happen to Nimi there? And to me?

33

WHEN THEY reached the edge of the forest, where they could already see the first village houses, Nehi said to them, Look, it's almost night. And they're worrying about you there. Go home, and if you want, you can come to our mountain hideaway sometimes. You can stay with us for a few hours, or a whole day, or more. Meanwhile, please be very careful not to catch that mocking and scoffing disease. Do just the opposite. Try gradually to get your friends, or at least some of them, out of the habit of taunting and teasing. Talk to them. And talk to the insulters and even the abusers and all the ones who take pleasure in other people's misfortunes. Please, both of you, talk to anyone who will listen. Try to talk even to the ones who make fun of you and condemn you and mock you.

Don't let them get to you, just try to tell them over and over again.

Until one day, there might be a change of heart, and then we'll come down from the mountain and maybe a new heart will be born in all the people and animals and birds, and all the meat-eaters will get used to eating beefberries instead of preying on other animals. And maybe all my friends and I and Nimi the Owl will be able to come out of the dense forest and return to the village and live our lives in our homes and yards and fields and caves and on the riverbank, and my desire for revenge will crumble and fall away from me like a snake's dry skin, and we'll work and love and take walks and sing and play and talk without preying on others or being preyed upon and without ridiculing each other. Now please go on your way. And don't forget. Even when you grow up and become parents to your own children, don't forget. Sleep well, Maya and Matti. Good night to you both.

As Maya and Matti came out of the dark forest, hand in hand, and walked towards the lights of the village, Matti said to Maya, We have to tell Almon. We have to tell Emanuella. We have to tell Danir.

Maya said, Not just them, Matti. We'll have to tell everyone. My mother. The old people. Your parents. And it won't be easy for us.

And Matti said: They'll probably say we have whoopitis.

And Maya said: And we have to find Nimi. We have to bring him back.

And Matti said: Tomorrow.